Rosie Goodwin is th[illegible] selling author of more than [illegible] he is the first author in the world to be[illegible] wed to follow three of Catherine Cookson's trilogies with her own sequels. Having worked in the social services sector for many years, then fostered a number of children, she is now a fulltime novelist. She is one of the top fifty most borrowed authors from UK libraries and has sold over four million copies across her career. Rosie lives in Nuneaton, the setting for many of her books, with her husband and their beloved dogs.

Rosie
GOODWIN

Sweet Charity

A Quick Reads Original

ZAFFRE

A Note for Readers

This Quick Read title, *Sweet Charity* by Rosie Goodwin, is set in 1890 – well over a hundred years ago. The main character, Charity, belongs to a group of people who are called 'Gypsies' in the book. Romani is another word used to describe this group known for their nomadic lifestyle – meaning they move around, rather than living in one fixed place. Charity is proud of her family, her culture and their traditions. She calls herself a Gypsy. 'Gypsy' is a legally recognised ethnic identity for Romani people, although some individuals prefer not to use the term.

Chapter One

1890

Above, the stars were twinkling in a dark velvet sky. The Gypsy girls' skirts twirled and shone like multicoloured jewels in the light from the campfire. They were dancing around it, laughing and enjoying themselves. But as Charity watched them, she had mixed feelings. This party was being held in celebration of her sixteenth birthday. The end of her childhood. That was a daunting thought. Up until now she had led a charmed life. The much-loved daughter of Jethro and Destiny, she had been pampered and spoiled, but she had also never known what it was to live in one place. The community travelled each year from one end of the country to another. The men found work where they could and their main income came from the horses they bred and raised. Charity's earliest memories were of watching the horses being led into the rivers. There, the Gypsy women and boys would wash them. Then they would brush their tails and manes until they gleamed. Once a year, in early June, they would travel to Appleby Fair in Westmorland. It was here that many of the horses were sold. It was one of Charity's favourite places. There, they would meet up with other Gypsy groups and friendships were formed.

The women also did what they could to earn money. Charity's grandmother had what she termed 'the gift' and would earn extra money telling people's fortunes. She also claimed that she could receive messages from the dead. Many people visited her hoping to hear from their dearly departed. Other Gypsy women made lace so fine that it looked like silken cobwebs. The lace sold for great sums of money to those that could afford it.

Charity loved the sense of freedom her life afforded her. She loved to run barefoot through long grass with her best friend, Scarlet. She loved the feeling of the wind in her hair. And she loved the vardo her family lived in. It was a gaily painted wagon on four wheels that contained everything a family needed to live in. In winter she and her brother Matthew lived inside it with their parents. They would sleep on little pull-out beds. A small pot-bellied stove that belched out smoke kept them all warm and cosy. In the summer they would sleep beneath the vardo with the dogs. They would bathe in the rivers and swim to their hearts' content, laughing and splashing. The river water would also be used to wash their clothes before they were hung on the hedgerows to dry. Charity had only a basic knowledge of reading and writing, but by the age of ten she could ride a horse bareback. She could find mushrooms and watercress and bake bread and milk a goat. She could also skin a rabbit and make a very tasty stew. To Charity it was an idyllic way of life, and all she'd ever known, but that was all set to change.

Once a Gypsy girl reached sixteen years of age, her parents would begin to look for a husband for her. It was this that was concerning Charity. She didn't feel ready to be married. Especially not to someone her parents chose. There was talk of it being her distant cousin Felix. For some time, the two families had hinted at a union between the two. Admittedly Felix was handsome. The trouble was he knew it, and Charity avoided him whenever she could. Even more so now because her heart belonged to another. Luca was the son of the ringmaster at a circus that also visited the area a few times a year. There had been a spark between them for some time. But the year before they had grown close. Before the Gypsies left they had shared a kiss. And ever since she hadn't been able to stop thinking of him.

'Charity!'

As she heard her father's voice calling her, her thoughts returned to the present. Jethro was standing on the steps of their vardo and she crossed to him.

A hush fell across the assembled crowd as Charity reached him.

'My loved one.' He smiled at her proudly as he handed her a gift. It was a beautiful small knife with an intricately carved mother of pearl handle. 'You must now wear this always in your garter to protect you from unwanted attention. Happy birthday. Today you become a woman.'

'Thank you, Papa.'

Charity inclined her head and, lifting her skirt, she placed the knife into her garter next to her skin. Such a gift was given to every Gypsy girl in Charity's community when they reached sixteen. From now on she would be forbidden to be alone with men or boys unless they were family. Jethro would shadow her and save her from unwanted attention until a suitable husband was found. This was one of the Gypsy traditions that Charity felt was unfair. The boys were allowed to pursue whoever they wanted, often leaving broken hearts behind in the towns they visited.

A cheer went up and with a sigh Charity returned to the party. It was her birthday after all.

Chapter Two

Luca hammered in the last tent peg on the guy ropes holding up the big top. He sat back on his heels and surveyed the activity going on around him. Everywhere was hustle and bustle as the circus folk prepared for the first show. He wiped the sweat from his brow and rose to his feet. Now that the enormous tent was up, he could start marking out the ring inside, and once that was done the benches would need to be moved into position. There was still a lot to do.

Luca had never known a life away from the circus, nor did he wish to. His great-grandfather had started the circus and it had been passed down through the family. His father, Rory, owned it now and one day soon it would be Luca's responsibility. Rory was getting old and was training Luca to take his place when the time was right. Luca would become the ringmaster then and be responsible for running the show. Not that the circus people needed much prompting. They each had a job to do and did it without needing to be told.

Next to the circus the small fair that travelled with them was also being erected. It was a more recent addition and had proved very popular. There were swing boats and a merry-go-round as well as many stalls. There was a smaller tent where the psychic, Gypsy May-Lee, would peer into her crystal ball and tell people their fortunes. It always amused Luca to see people queuing to see her. He had no idea if Gypsy May-Lee really did have a gift but her punters rarely left disappointed. Another tent housed the bearded lady, although Luca knew that the beard was glued on. The coconut shy was another popular attraction for the visitors.

Behind the fancy costumes and the glamour there was a life of hard work, but Luca didn't mind that. In fact, he still got a thrill each night when the lights were dimmed. He loved to see the reactions when the performances began. Cocoman the clown would always open the show. He would parade around the ring squirting children with his water pistol. They would squeal with delight at his huge red nose and enormous shoes. And then Luca's father would appear in his ringmaster's top hat and tails to wild applause. The timings for the show had to be accurate, and they always were. There were trapeze artists and jugglers. There was Fernando the fire-eater, and not forgetting the live animals they had tamed and trained. Luca played a big role in caring for the animals. He loved each and every one of them. They had bears, performing horses and dogs. There were also two magnificent tigers. The audience would gasp with fear and admiration when they were led into the ring. At one point they had even had an elephant. Sadly, when he grew old, they had retired him to live out the rest of his life in a zoo. Rory had always insisted that the animals should have as good a life as possible. Luca agreed with him and cared for them each day, feeding them and cleaning out their enclosures.

Now, Luca's eyes moved to the next field. The circus came to Nuneaton twice a year and usually Rory's good friend, Jethro, would join them. He and his Gypsy camp would set up in the next field over. Rory and Jethro had been good friends since they were boys. Now Luca and Jethro's son, Matthew, were firm friends too. Originally, Rory's father had bought some horses for training from Jethro's father and they would try to meet up three or four times a year. This year, though, there was no sign of Jethro yet, so Luca entered the big top to begin on the ring.

As he worked, Luca's thoughts turned to Charity, Matthew's sister. For many years she had trailed around after Luca and Matthew and they'd found her to be a bit of a nuisance. She could climb a tree as well as they could. She could swim like a fish. But she had been childish and annoying. But then two years ago, when the circus and the Gypsy camp met at Appleby Fair, Charity had emerged from her vardo and Luca's eyes had almost popped out of his head. She was like a butterfly emerging from a cocoon. The puppy fat had been replaced by womanly curves. Her dark hair, normally yanked back into an unflattering ponytail, was loose and shining. It hung across her shoulders like a satin cloak and her eyes sparkled. Luca, like most of the circus boys, had had his fair share of girls. They flocked around them, and Luca had always had his pick, but they were easily forgotten. From that moment on, Charity was not. Matthew had noticed the way his friend looked at her and had frowned.

'You know it wouldn't do for you to grow fond of my sister,' he'd warned. 'She is a Gypsy and expected to marry one of her own kind.'

Luca blushed with embarrassment. No girl had ever made him feel that way before.

'I'm aware of that,' he had answered coldly. But still, he hadn't been able to take his eyes off her. It was as if she had cast a spell over him and now he could hardly wait to see her again.

Chapter Three

The Gypsies pulled onto the field at the side of the circus later that day. The evening performance was in full swing and the big top was full of applause and laughter.

Luca had made a point during the show of popping out to see if there was a sight of them. When he did see the vardos arriving his heart did a little flip. He hurried back inside. There would be no time to welcome them until the performance was over. And even then, it would have to wait. This evening it was his turn to work the swing boats, which were so popular with the visiting children.

The evening seemed to pass so slowly. Luca's eyes kept straying to the Gypsy camp, but as yet there was no sign of Charity. At last, the crowd began to disperse and the fair became quiet. Luca quickly tied the swing boats down and took the evening's earnings to his father. Only then did he have time to visit the camp.

He found Matthew sitting beside a campfire eating his supper; sausages with potatoes.

Matthew stood up and slapped him on the back and shook his hand as he greeted him. 'Hello, Luca, it's good to see you.'

Luca smiled as he returned the greeting but his eyes were searching for Charity. There was no sign of her although he spotted her friend Scarlet, who flashed him a smile.

'So how are you all?'

Matthew nodded. 'We're well, and yourself?'

'I'm very well.'

'I think we have a couple of horses your father will be interested in.' Matthew gestured towards a corner of the field where the horses were tethered. They were grazing contentedly.

'We have one pure white foal and a palomino. She is superb! My father has kept them to give your father first chance.' He kissed his fingers. 'Her coat is like spun gold and her mane and tail are pure white.'

'I'm sure my father will be interested to see them,' Luca assured him. 'But where are the rest of the family?'

Matthew pointed over his shoulder. 'My mother has been unwell. Charity is seeing to her needs and my father is directing the last vardos into the camp.'

Luca felt strangely disappointed. If this was the case it was unlikely he would catch up with Charity that evening. Still, there was always tomorrow. He would look forward to it. He took a seat on the ground cross-legged beside his friend. They talked about the places they had visited and the things they had done since the last time they met.

The next morning, Matthew and his father left the camp early. It was cattle market day in the town. They took four of the horses they were hoping to sell. The market was always busy. Farmers from the farms surrounding the town would congregate with animals they wished to sell. There would be cages and pens full of pigs, cows, sheep, geese, chickens and ducks as well as horses. When bartering for the animals was finished, the farmers would go for a well-earned tankard of ale in the market tavern. Luca had no doubt the Gypsies would join them, which meant they could be gone for most of the day. It also meant that he might see Charity at the camp. Quickly, he went to see to the needs of the circus animals before wandering towards the vardos. And then he saw her. His heart skipped a beat. She was in the corner of the field brushing the horses with some of the other girls.

Charity spotted him as he came towards her and a flush rose to her cheeks. Over the last couple of years, he had changed a lot as well. He had been a lanky, skinny boy, but with hard work and a life in the fresh air he had grown into a very handsome young man. He was wearing an open-necked shirt with the sleeves rolled up to his elbows. His skin was golden brown and she could see the muscles rippling in his arms.

'Hello, Charity.'

As he stopped before her, she realised he had also grown taller. He now towered over her.

'Hello, Luca. How are you?'

Once she would have thrown her arms about him and given him a hug. But that would be frowned upon now she was sixteen.

'Do you fancy a stroll by the river?' Luca asked.

Charity bit her lip. Did she dare? But then she reasoned that her father and Matthew would be gone for some time and her mother was still in the vardo feeling unwell. What harm could it do?

She nodded and they set off side by side. Once they were out of sight of the camp, they relaxed a little. They began to feel more at ease with each other.

They were strolling along the banks of the River Anker. Charity stopped to sit on the grass beneath the branches of a weeping willow and dangled her feet in the cool water.

'So how have you been?'

As Luca turned to watch her, she thought of the kiss they had shared and she flushed again. There was a strange fluttering feeling in her stomach that she had never had before.

'I've been well,' she answered quietly. She was very conscious of his closeness. Their arms were almost touching and she wished they would. 'I had my birthday. My sixteenth birthday, so Papa will be looking for a husband for me now.'

Luca scowled as he plucked a blade of glass and began to chew on it. It was the worst news he could have received. He realised that the thought of Charity with another man made him jealous in a way he never had been before.

'And how do you feel about that?'

Charity shrugged as she tossed her long dark hair across her shoulder. 'I'm not happy about it,' she admitted. 'But this is our custom. All Gypsy girls are expected to wed once they reach sixteen.'

'But you can't!' The words burst from him before he could stop them.

Shocked, she faced him. 'What did you just say?'

Luca gulped and mopped his forehead feeling foolish. 'I'm sorry . . . I shouldn't have said that.'

She was staring deep into his eyes and it was his turn to flush now.

'But why?' she whispered.

'Because I can't bear to think of you with anyone else. I've thought of you every single day since we last met.'

'And I have thought of you,' she admitted breathlessly.

As one, they moved towards each other and Luca's lips came down on hers. She didn't try to stop him or push him away. Suddenly it was as if they were the only two people left in the whole world. Their arms tightened about each other and it was a long time before they pulled apart. When they finally did, they stared at each other, breathless. Something had been awakened in them as they realised that they loved each other.

Luca was beaming. He knew what the strange feelings he had been suffering were now. No other girl had ever made him feel as Charity did. And he suspected no other ever would. She was the girl for him.

'So, problem solved.' He was beaming now. 'If your father wants you to marry you can marry me!'

His smile died as he saw the stricken look on her face.

'But you know the Gypsy traditions.' Her eyes filled with tears as she shook her head sadly. 'My papa likes you, Luca, but he would never allow such a union. I must wed one of our own kind. He must have Gypsy blood flowing through his veins. You live with the circus. You have your own traditions.'

'Does he have someone in mind for you?' Luca was seething with jealousy now. Why hadn't he realised before that Charity was the one for him?

'I think so,' she admitted miserably. 'I have a distant cousin. We will be seeing him and his family at Appleby Fair in June. I think the marriage will be arranged between our families then.'

'And do you like him?'

Charity shook her head. 'No, I don't.'

'But you can't be expected to marry someone you don't even like!' Luca was appalled.

She rose and dusted down her colourful skirts. Time was moving on and she was afraid of being missed.

'We must go back. We will talk of this again.'

'When?' He rose to stand beside her and took her hand.

She gently pulled away. 'I don't know. But please, we must go back. I will go ahead of you in case my parents see us coming back.'

He stood and watched her helplessly as she left.

Chapter Four

It was the following evening before they were able to steal another moment together. The men had gone into town for a drink at the inn. Charity's mother was still unwell and fast asleep in the vardo, so Charity lifted her shawl and crept quietly away into the darkness. Luca spotted her almost instantly. He had barely taken his eyes off her vardo, hoping for a sight of her. The fair was deserted now and the last of the visitors had long gone, but he had stayed up, picking litter.

'I can't be long. Papa might return soon,' she told him in a hushed voice. He nodded. Every single stolen moment with her was precious.

'Has any more been said about finding you a husband?' he asked. He had hardly slept the night before for worrying about it.

'When I was outside preparing our meal this evening, I heard my parents talking.' She sighed as she hugged her shawl to her. 'It is as I thought. They have my cousin in mind for me. They will speak to his parents at Appleby Fair.'

'But it's so unfair,' Luca growled. 'Surely they would understand if we told them how we feel about each other. We are not so very different. We both live on the road, travelling from place to place.'

'I think you would find your parents would be against it too if they knew.' Charity shook her head. 'I am sure they will have someone in mind for you as well. It's only because you are a man that they haven't suggested you settling down yet.'

They had reached the hedge bordering the field now. Luca gathered her into his arms.

'So how long will you be staying here?'

'Your father has gone with mine to decide on a payment for the two horses. The palomino and the white one. Then we will probably move on.'

At that moment they heard the sound of laughter floating across the field. It was the men returning and Charity panicked. Gypsy girls knew better than to disobey their parents.

'I must go.'

She was off like the wind, her long hair flying behind her. Luca stayed in the shelter of the hedge. He didn't move again until he saw that Charity was safely back inside the vardo. Only then did he stuff his hands into his pockets and make his way back to his own trailer.

The next morning, Luca and his father collected the two horses. As Jethro had said, they were magnificent. Luca knew that he would enjoy training them to perform in the ring.

'We are invited to a meal tonight at the Gypsy camp once the fair is closed. They will be moving on tomorrow,' Luca's father informed him.

Luca's heart sank. On the surrounding farms the farmers would be employing men to plant their potatoes. They also employed people to fell trees when needed. It was a job the Gypsies did each year and now they were keen to get started. Then in June they would move on to Appleby Fair. If, as Charity and Luca feared, her parents did arrange a marriage then Luca and Charity's relationship would be over. Over before it had even started, Luca thought bitterly.

Thoughts buzzed around in Luca's head like bees until he felt dizzy. But suddenly it was time for the matinee circus performance and he had to concentrate on that. Once it was over he had to feed the animals. They would rest then until the evening performance when it would all begin once more. The remainder of the day passed slowly and Luca was glad when the fair began to grow quiet. His parents were in their trailer preparing to go for a meal with Charity's parents. They usually had a get-together on the night before the Gypsies moved on and it often ended up in a party. Luca really wasn't in the mood but he would go. It was a chance to see Charity, and who knew, they might even be able to snatch a few moments alone.

Chapter Five

The circus folk and the Gypsies were gathered about an enormous campfire. The women were roasting meat and the men were drinking ale from the barrels that had been rolled out. Luca had washed and changed into his best shirt. His hair was still damp and as Charity spotted him, she thought how handsome he looked. The children were racing about and rolling on the grass. The Gypsy dogs were prowling looking for bones and the atmosphere was light. Laughter floated on the air but Luca barely noticed anything or anyone but Charity. Her long dark hair and the gold hoops she wore in her ears gleamed in the glow of the fire. She was so beautiful that she almost took his breath away. Somewhere, someone was playing a fiddle and the Gypsy girls were dancing around the fire.

'Luca, come and join us, son,' Luca's father called to him. He was standing with Charity's father and Luca made his way towards them. 'So, what do you think of the new horses?' His father valued Luca's opinion.

Someone pressed a mug of ale into Luca's hand and he nodded his thanks. 'They're both beautiful creatures. But I think the palomino will take some training. She's very spirited.'

His father laughed and clapped him on the shoulder. 'If anyone can train her, you can,' he said. He was proud of his son; Luca had always had a way with horses. With all animals if it came to that, and his father had every confidence in him.

As they stood there, Scarlet sidled up to them. She was the daughter of Madame Fifi, who showed the horses in the ring and she and Charity had been best friends who had spent their summers playing together. They had shared all their hopes and dreams. That was until Charity confided in her about her feelings for Luca. Scarlet was very beautiful. Her hair was as red as the flames in the fire and her eyes were a deep green. Young men flocked to her like moths around a flame. She could have had her pick of any she wanted, but there was only one man in her sights. She and Luca had grown up together. She was just one year younger than him and had always thought that one day she would be his bride and now she was seething with jealousy.

'Shall we join the dance?' She fluttered her eyelashes at Luca.

When he shook his head, the smile slid from her face. 'Perhaps later?' She swung around and marched away, her pride wounded.

From the shelter of a vardo Scarlet kept a close watch on Luca. There would be no sneaking off with Charity that night if she could prevent it. She just wished the morning could come quickly now so that the Gypsies would leave.

Within an hour the ale was flowing like water and many of the men were merry. Apart from Luca, who had kept a low profile as his eyes followed Charity about. Eventually, they managed to make their way towards each other.

'Shall we take a walk by the brook?' Luca whispered.

Charity glanced towards Jethro; luckily he was still talking to Luca's father.

She nodded. 'Yes, but let me go first. You follow in a couple of minutes.' Without even looking at him she drew her shawl about her and slipped away.

Luca waited, the minutes dragging by, before following silently. Charity was waiting for him by the stream and they instantly moved into each other's arms. It was dark by then, so there was little chance of them being seen. Or so they thought.

'Oh . . . hello, you two.'

Scarlet's voice made them spring guiltily apart. They hadn't heard her approach.

'What are you doing here?' Scarlet asked innocently. Inside, she was burning with jealousy but it wouldn't do to let them see that.

'Oh, I just fancied a stroll along the banks of the stream,' Luca told her. 'And it seems that Charity had the same idea.'

Scarlet flashed him a smile. 'That makes three of us then. Shall we walk together?'

When she moved on, Charity and Luca had no choice but to follow her. They walked some way in silence until Scarlet said, 'Shall we sit down on the grass for a while? We could dangle our feet in the stream.'

'Actually, I think I might head back now.' Charity was upset that she and Luca had been robbed of these few precious moments together.

'It looks like it's just you and me in that case.' Scarlet smiled winningly at Luca again and he glanced at Charity helplessly.

It would look too obvious if he were to refuse. He watched Charity stride away, her bright skirts swirling around her, before reluctantly taking a seat on the grass beside Scarlet.

She moved close to him and pulled her skirts above her knees. She was showing a pretty pair of ankles but Luca didn't notice. He was too busy watching Charity being swallowed up by the darkness.

'Do you remember how we used to do this when we were children?'

Scarlet's voice dragged Luca's thoughts back to her as she dipped her feet into the cold water.

'Yes, yes I do.'

She could see that he was distracted and pouted prettily. 'I hope I didn't disturb anything between you two?'

He shook his head. 'No, of course you didn't,' he lied.

'Good.' She stared at him. 'Because you must know nothing could come of you and Charity wanting to be together. We are circus people, Luca, and Charity is a Gypsy. We marry our own kind.'

He jumped effortlessly to his feet and looked down at her.

'I don't know why. We're not so very different from them. We both live travelling lives.'

She shrugged. 'Even so, that's how it is and has been since the dawn of time. It is our tradition. Perhaps you should look for a suitable wife amongst your own kind.'

He shook his head. 'I think it's too late for that.' And without another word he marched away leaving Scarlet with tears in her eyes.

After hurrying through the darkness, Luca saw Charity just about to enter her parents' vardo. She saw him coming and paused.

'Wait for me later tonight down by the stream,' she whispered. 'I'll slip out when my parents are asleep. They'll be drunk by then and probably won't even notice.'

He nodded and walked away.

Later, down by the stream, it was the early hours of the morning before he heard her soft tread on the grass behind him. Everywhere was quiet save for the sound of the night creatures. The giant bonfire was nothing more than ash and embers now. The party was long over and the camp was deserted.

'I was beginning to think you weren't coming.' He rushed towards her and took her in his arms. He had been on his feet since early the previous morning and he was exhausted. But he would have waited all night for her if need be. This might be their last chance to be together.

'What are we going to do?' she asked forlornly.

He sighed. 'I don't know but we must think of something. I can't bear the thought of you being promised to someone else.' And then their lips touched and the world seemed to stand still. That night on the banks of the stream the two became one.

'I'm so sorry, I shouldn't have done that,' Luca fretted when it was over and she lay in his arms. She shook her head. 'Don't be sorry, I'm not.' She had given him that which should have been saved for her husband. She had no regrets. It had felt like the most natural thing in the world.

'But what shall we do now?'

'If it means us being together I must run away,' she told him solemnly.

'And become my wife?'

She nodded. 'I think I would like that. I am already yours now.'

Charity stroked his hair. 'My family and I will leave for Appleby Fair in the morning. You and the circus will join us within the next month. While we are there, I will be going into town to buy provisions. When I'm there I'll try to find a job and somewhere to stay in the surrounding villages. On a farm perhaps or in a shop. I cannot remain with my parents now. They would disown me if they knew what I'd done. And anyway, we must be together. So, before they can announce who they wish me to marry I must slip away. Somehow, before my people move on, I'll get word to Scarlet of where I'll be. Then when the circus leaves Appleby you can come to join me. We'll have to make a life away from our people if we are to be together.'

Luca nodded in agreement as he drew her to her feet. It would be a wrench for him to leave his people. He loved his life in the circus, but he loved Charity more. They adjusted their clothing and hand in hand made their way back to the camp.

'I shall count the days until I see you again. And please be careful,' he whispered.

She nodded as they shared one last kiss. And then she crept back into her parents' vardo. The decision had been made.

Chapter Six

The next morning, at first light, the Gypsy camp was a hive of activity. The men were preparing the horses for the long journey. The women were packing the vardos and cooking a meal for them to have before they left. It might be late in the day before they ate again.

Luca glimpsed Charity a few times but there was no time to talk. By mid-morning the Gypsies were ready to leave. The horses that would pull the vardos were harnessed and attached. The horses that would be sold at the fair were tethered behind. Luca's and Charity's fathers said their goodbyes. And then the long line of vardos left to embark on the journey.

As Charity's vardo passed Luca they exchanged no more than a glance. Charity's mother was sitting beside her and they didn't want to raise suspicion. Luca felt as if his heart was being torn from his chest. It would be only a matter of weeks until he saw the girl he loved again. And yet it felt like a lifetime.

Finally, the last vardo was gone and the place felt strangely quiet. Luca found it hard to concentrate on anything, especially as Scarlet seemed to be behind him every time he turned around.

Later that day, Luca had been training the new horses in a field.Scarlet hung over the fence beaming at him.

'Would you like to go for a walk this evening?' she called. 'I mean after the fair is finished.'

Luca frowned and shook his head. 'No, I think I might have an early night.'

Just for a moment, Scarlet scowled. He hadn't been too tired to go walking with Charity the night before. 'Then perhaps you'd like to come to our vardo for supper?' She smiled prettily at him. 'I'm making a rabbit stew. It's one of your favourites.'

Again, Luca shook his head. 'Thanks, but like I said, I'm a bit tired.'

Scarlet didn't believe a word of it. Luca was one of the most hard-working young men in the circus. More like pining for Charity, she thought spitefully. Even so, she kept her smile fixed firmly in place. That morning Charity had confided to her the plan she and Luca had made to be together. Now Scarlet had only a few weeks to get him to focus on her rather than Charity. She was used to young men flocking around her for attention. And whatever she had to do, she was determined that Luca would be one of them.

It was customary for the circus men to bathe in the river after the fair had closed, and so late that night Luca made his way there. He had waited until all was quiet. He wasn't in the mood for company. Luckily, the riverbank was deserted when he arrived and so he quickly stripped his clothes off and dived in. The cold water closed around him and after swimming a few yards he turned on his back to float. High above the sky was studded with stars but he barely noticed. He was thinking of Charity and wondering what she was doing. He was so immersed in his thoughts that it was some time before he saw a shape on the river-bank. It was a person and whoever it was, they were stripping their clothes off. Assuming it was one of the circus lads Luca looked away. As he turned back and the moon sailed from behind the clouds, he was horrified to see Scarlet swimming towards him. She was quite naked and smiling at him. With an oath he struck out for the riverbank.

'What do you think you're doing?' He was so angry it was hard not to shout. 'If your father found us here naked together he'd go mad.'

She laughed as she swam towards him. 'So he would. He'd probably order you to marry me now you've seen me like this. But would that be such a bad thing?'

Luca climbed out of the river and snatched up his shirt to cover himself. As Scarlet climbed out beside him, he couldn't help but notice how beautiful she was. Her breasts were full and high and her waist was tiny, her legs long and shapely. Even so his heart belonged to another and he turned his back on her. He began to yank his clothes on as she reached out to him.

'Don't you like what you see?' Her voice was seductive but he wasn't tempted.

'You're a beautiful girl, Scarlet, but you know I love Charity. She told me she'd confided in you.'

She scowled. 'Yes, she did. But you and I both know nothing can ever come of that. Her people and ours would never allow it.'

He shrugged as he hastily buttoned his trousers, averting his eyes.

'We'll find a way,' he told her. And without another word, he hurried away leaving Scarlet with just her anger for company.

Chapter Seven

They had been at Appleby Fair for a week but it had felt like a year to Charity. Every day she had fretted that this might be the day that her father announced who he wanted her to marry.

She had been shopping in the town on a few occasions now, and despite asking around, as yet she had had no luck finding a job or a place for her and Luca to live. Still, she consoled herself, there was plenty of time. The circus wouldn't be arriving for another two or three weeks at least. She was missing Luca every minute of every day. Her mother had noticed that she was quiet and not her usual self. Charity had told her she thought she was coming down with a cold and she had accepted that. During the day many deals had been struck. People came from miles around to view the livestock. They had been so busy that the daylight hours seemed to have passed in a blur. The young men frequently bathed the horses in the river until their coats gleamed. Then, when they emerged, the girls were kept busy braiding the horses' manes and brushing their tails. Charity was doing this one day when Felix, her cousin, approached her. His black hair curled on his shoulders and he was bare chested. His skin was golden brown and his arms heavily muscled.

'Good day,' he greeted her. 'I hear your family and mine are to throw a party next week.'

Charity's heart sank. This would likely be when their fathers were planning to announce their betrothal.

'Good day, Felix.' She tried to stay calm. He liked what he saw if the way he was looking at her was anything to go by – like she was one of his horses. She chewed on her lip. Just one week to find somewhere to escape to. She must be gone before the announcement was made. Otherwise, it would bring shame on both families. Tomorrow she would double her efforts.

The next morning Charity set off bright and early. Luckily, her mother needed some things from the town. Instead of heading towards the shops, though, she set off for Orton. It was a small pretty market town a few miles from Appleby. After a good walk she began to approach the farms and small holdings she passed. At each one she enquired if there were any jobs going.

Some, seeing her brightly coloured Gypsy clothing, shooed her away. Others merely shook their heads, and she began to become down-hearted. By lunchtime she'd had no luck at all and she turned to begin the journey back. It wouldn't do for her to be gone for too long. It might arouse suspicion. The sun was beating down by that time and she was hot and thirsty.

She passed a small farmhouse where she saw a man feeding pigs in a sty. She opened the gate to the farmyard and approached him. He stared at her suspiciously before asking, 'What can I do for you?' His voice was not friendly.

'I'm looking for work.'

He frowned as he eyed her up and down.

'Aren't you a Gypsy? One of those from Appleby Fair?'

She nodded. 'Yes, I am. But I wish to find work and leave them.'

He scratched his head. 'And what sort of job is it you're after?'

'I'm willing to do anything,' she told him hastily. 'Housework, farm work, whatever you have. I'm a good worker.' Suddenly she was hopeful. At least he hadn't immediately turned her away.

He scratched his head as he looked across the yard to the farmhouse. He was quite a young man, somewhere in his thirties, she judged, and he had a kind face, although he looked weary.

'Well . . .' He paused. 'I could do with someone to mind my children and keep house. I lost my wife last year and it's been difficult. I have a woman from the village come in twice a week. She does some washing and cleaning for me, but it's not enough really. I have the farm to run and the children are alone for much of the time. Would you be willing to live in? I couldn't pay you too much.'

Charity nodded eagerly.

He seemed to think about it for a moment before saying, 'When could you start?'

'Tomorrow. Would that be soon enough?'

He nodded and pointed towards the farmhouse. 'You'd best come and meet the children in that case.'

They picked their way across the yard where chickens were pecking amongst the cobbles.

The first thing Charity noticed when they entered a large kitchen was how unloved it looked. Dirty pots were piled high in the sink and every piece of furniture was coated with dust. Two small children were sitting at a table.

'That's Tilly, she's two, and that's Simon, he's four,' he introduced them.

They were nice-looking children but Charity thought both were in need of a good bath.

They eyed her warily as she approached and bent to their level. 'Hello, I'm Charity.'

They were both blue-eyed and blonde-haired and were chewing on crusts of dry bread.

'I'm not much of a cook,' he said quietly and Charity felt sorry for him. 'And the house . . .' He spread his hands in defeat. 'I'm afraid I'm not very good at housework either. My Mary kept this place shiny as a new pin. Have you had any experience of caring for children?'

'Oh yes,' she assured him. 'We Gypsy girls are taught to look after children from a young age.'

He shrugged. 'Very well. I suppose we could give it a trial.'

She smiled. 'Thank you. I'll be here early tomorrow morning.'

She left with a feeling of relief. Now all she had to do was wait until the camp was asleep and escape. Then when the circus arrived, she would get word to Luca where she was. And their new life together could begin.

Chapter Eight

'You have been gone a long time!' Charity's mother scolded when she arrived back at the camp. She had bought the shopping her mother needed on the way.

'Yes, I'm sorry. I got carried away looking in the shops.' She hated lying but what choice did she have?

The rest of the day passed painfully slowly. Charity was feeling a mixture of emotions. There was sadness at the thought of leaving her parents and the life she had known. She felt anxious about what might lie ahead. But overriding everything was her need to be with Luca.

During the afternoon, her mother went outside to cook over the campfire. While she was gone, Charity hastily packed her belongings into a pillowcase and wrote her family a note admitting that she had met someone she loved and telling them not to worry about her. When she was finished, she hid them beneath her small pallet bed. Then all she had to do was wait for her chance to leave.

Luckily, the Gypsies retired early that evening. The men had had a busy day tending the horses and the women had been busy cooking. They were all tired. Soon after they had all settled in their beds, Charity's family's snores echoed around the vardo. Charity had gone to bed fully clothed and lay awake until she was sure they were all fast asleep. Only then did she quietly rise and retrieve her bundle. Then she looked down on them all with tears in her eyes as she placed the note on the table where they would find it. Once she left there could be no coming back. The shame of what she was about to do would mean that they would disown her. Even so, what she felt for Luca was strong, so very quietly she slipped away. She paused once at the edge of the camp to look back at the vardo. It had been the only home she had ever known, but it was time to start the next chapter of her life.

She reached the farmhouse in the early hours of the morning and saw that it was in darkness. She had no wish to disturb the farmer so she crept into the barn. She made herself a bed of hay and lay down to sleep with the chickens. When the farmer rose with the dawn, he found her sitting on the doorstep.

'Ah . . .' He looked mildly surprised to see her. He hadn't been at all sure that she would turn up. He looked embarrassed as he stood aside and she stepped past him. 'I'm sorry, I forgot to ask you your name.'

She dropped her bundle onto a chair. 'My name is Charity.'

'Right, and I'm Eddie. Eddie Wells, and this is Top Acres Farm. I was just about to put the kettle on for some tea.'

'I'll do that,' she volunteered. 'If you'll just show me where everything is.' She supposed she should start as she meant to go on.

He was embarrassed as he pointed to the sink. 'I'm afraid most of the pots are in there. I was going to wash them last night, but I never got around to it. What with seeing to the children and one thing and another. The kettle is on the hob.'

Charity had only ever cooked or boiled water over a fire before. Still, she was sure she would soon get used to it. While she was waiting for the kettle to boil, she washed some mugs. She carried them to the table before asking, 'Where do you keep the milk?'

'There's a pantry to the side of the sink. That door there.' He pointed. 'And when I've milked the cows, I'll bring you some fresh in.'

'I could take that job on for you,' she offered. She was used to milking a goat. Surely milking a cow would not be that much different.

'Really?' He looked relieved. It was a job his wife had always done before she passed away.

Soon, they were seated with steaming mugs of tea in front of them.

'So where will I be sleeping?' Charity asked.

He nodded to another door that led to some stairs. 'There are three bedrooms up there. I sleep in one, the children sleep in another and you can have the third. I'm afraid it will need cleaning though.'

'That's no problem. I'll tackle it later on.'

The children came downstairs soon after. They eyed Charity warily as she ushered them to the table, but when she served them with bowls of sweetened porridge they actually smiled. Since their mother had died their staple diet had been stale bread and jam.

When they had eaten, Charity set about cleaning the kitchen. Her own room could wait until later. Mid-morning she stopped cleaning to prepare a meal. The children had gone out to play in the sunshine and when they came in for their lunch, they eyed the meal hungrily. Charity had made them a cottage pie. She had been out into the vegetable garden and fetched a cabbage too. Eddie was still out in the fields working so she'd warm his in the oven when he came in. The children cleared their plates, mopping them clean with the last of the stale bread. Bellies full, they went back out into the sun to play while Charity finished cleaning the kitchen. As yet, they had barely spoken to her although they were smiling at her now.

Eddie arrived home late afternoon and stared around in amazement. The whole kitchen seemed to be sparkling. The windows had been washed and the floor mopped. She had taken the rugs outside and beaten all of the dust out of them. The sink was no longer full of dirty pots and the dinner she was warming for him in the oven smelled delicious. His stomach rumbled in anticipation. She had even found time to bake a fresh batch of bread. While he ate, she left him to have some time with the children, who had just come back in from the yard. She went up to look at her room. It was small but adequate and she set about making the bed up with clean sheets, before dusting and mopping the floor.

It wasn't until much later that evening when she went to bed exhausted that the tears came. She was missing her parents and her own little bed. It would be the first night she had ever been apart from them. She was homesick, but there was no turning back. She just hoped in time that they would forgive her.

Her thoughts turned to Luca. Very soon now he would be arriving in Appleby with the circus. She could hardly wait to see him. But first she would have to try and get her address to Scarlet, and then her life with Luca could begin. She could hardly wait.

Chapter Nine

Charity had been at Top Acre Farm for two days when the kitchen door opened and a woman walked in. They stared at each other for a moment.

'Hello,' the woman said eventually, with a frown. 'Who are you?'

'I'm Charity. Mr Wells hired me to help look after the children and the house.'

'Oh, I see. Well, I'm Maureen. I come in twice a week to do the washing and help where I can.'

'Ah yes, Mr Wells did say.' Charity smiled at her. The woman looked to be in her thirties. She had fair hair tied back in an unbecoming bun on the back of her head. Her clothes were dowdy, grey from head to foot. But Charity could see that she could be attractive if she took a little more care of herself.

The woman looked around the room suspiciously. 'You've certainly made a difference in here,' she commented. 'Unfortunately, I never have time to get everything done.'

The children ran in at that moment and threw their arms about Maureen's waist. It was clear to see that they were fond of her and her face softened.

'So have you known Mr Wells long?' Charity asked as she filled the kettle at the sink.

The woman nodded. 'Oh yes. Many years. In fact . . .' She blushed. 'At one time Eddie and I were walking out together but then . . . Well, my father died and I have an invalid mother. I had to take on running the house and caring for her and my younger siblings.'

When Charity looked bemused, she went on, 'I think Eddie just got tired of waiting. And then he met Mary, his late wife.' She shrugged. 'And that was that. They were very happy together though.'

Charity could hear the sadness in her voice and felt sorry for her.

'But what is a lovely young woman like you doing here?' Maureen was curious now.

Charity looked away. 'Actually, my parents were about to announce my engagement to my cousin. I am of Gypsy stock and it's our custom, but I didn't want to marry him so . . .'

'So you ran away?' Maureen looked sympathetic.

Charity nodded.

'Was it because you love someone else?'

Charity bit her lip wondering if she could trust this woman and decided that she'd risk it.

'Yes, and hopefully he will come for me soon. I was wondering if Mr Wells might find him a job to do. And then perhaps we could carry on living here for a time.'

'I see.' Maureen took her shawl off and threw it over the back of a chair. As Charity made the tea, Maureen looked at her colourful clothes. They were grimy now after all the cleaning she had done.

'Don't you have any suitable work clothes?' she asked as Charity carried her drink to her.

Charity shook her head. 'No, unfortunately I don't. And the things I brought with me are all dirty now.'

'Well, I can help you there. Eddie told me I was welcome to take any of Mary's clothes I wanted. You're about the same size so there's bound to be something more suitable for you. I'll show you where they are in a minute.'

Charity looked dubious. 'But won't Mr Wells be upset seeing me in them?' she queried.

Maureen chuckled. 'I doubt it very much. Men don't tend to notice what we're wearing.'

When they had finished their drinks, Maureen led her upstairs. There was a large trunk in one corner of the front bedroom. She began to lift out skirts and blouses. They were very plain compared to what Charity was used to, but they were much more practical.

'I'll go and get changed right away,' Charity said gratefully.

'Yes, and I'd better go out to the wash house and start on the washing. I've no doubt there'll be a pile there waiting for me. I'll wash those clothes you're wearing for you as well if you like.'

Charity smiled and hurried away to get changed.

By lunchtime, Maureen had all the washing blowing in the wind on the lines strung across the yard.

Charity was in the kitchen preparing them all a light lunch of bread and cheese. Maureen had just sat down at the table when Eddie walked in. Charity saw the way the woman's eyes lit up at the sight of him. She knew in that moment that Maureen still loved him and thought how sad it was. She must be a very kind woman to sacrifice her own life for her family as she had.

'Ah, Maureen,' he greeted her. 'You've met Charity I see.'

Maureen nodded. 'I have indeed and she's doing a grand job from what I can see of it.' She looked slightly concerned. 'But will you still be needing me to come in now?'

He frowned at her. 'Of course I will. Charity is doing quite a few jobs about the farm now. That's as well as seeing to the children and the cleaning. I'm sure there's more than enough work to keep you both busy.'

She looked relieved.

'And how did Sadie's wedding go on Saturday?' he asked next.

'Really well and she looked beautiful. I can't believe she's the last of the young ones to leave. There's just me and Mother now. But she's growing weaker by the day,' she said sadly.

'And have you thought what you'll do when her time comes?' he asked gently.

Maureen shrugged. 'I dare say I'll try and get a full-time job somewhere.' She was also aware that she would have to leave her home. The last of her siblings had left, and she would be unable to pay the rent without their wages. She had hoped that she could move into the farm when she lost her mother. She would have loved to care for Eddie and the children. But if Charity stayed it seemed that she had that job now.

Charity went out to see to the animals after lunch while Maureen prepared an evening meal. Charity had enjoyed having another woman for company and was pleased when Maureen told her that she would be back the next day to tackle the ironing. They had clearly taken to each other. Once Maureen had left, as always, Charity's thoughts turned to Luca. She was counting the days until the circus arrived in Appleby. She was missing him even more than she had imagined she would. She missed her parents and her friends too, but if that was the price she would have to pay to be with Luca, she would gladly pay it.

Chapter Ten

As the last circus wagon pulled onto the road, Luca sighed with relief. It was very early in the morning but he didn't mind as, at last, they were on their way to Appleby Fair. Soon he would see Charity again and he could hardly wait. They had a long journey ahead of them but he didn't care. At least while they were on the road, he would be spared Scarlet's attentions. She had been like his shadow ever since the Gypsies had moved on. So much so that even his parents had noticed.

'I reckon she sees herself as wife material,' his father had teased him. 'Perhaps you should consider it?'

Luca wasn't amused. There was only one girl for him, but he couldn't tell his father that. He had been in a constant state of concern. Had Charity managed to make her escape? And if she had, was she somewhere safe? There was no way of knowing until he reached Appleby Fair and Charity got a message to Scarlet. And even then, the first two days would be busy erecting the big top and the fair. He steered the old horse pulling his trailer onto the road and tried to concentrate.

At that moment, in Top Acre Farm, Charity was lighting the fire in the kitchen. For the last few days, she had felt unwell, although she had no idea why. Her breasts were tender too and she found that the thought of breakfast made her feel nauseous. Soon Eddie and the children joined her.

'Are you feeling all right?' he asked kindly. 'You look a little pale.'

She nodded as she spooned porridge into the children's dishes. 'I think I might have caught a chill or something,' she answered.

'Then have an easy day,' he suggested. 'Maureen will be here shortly. She'll take over and look after the children.'

'Oh, there's no need for that,' she assured him. 'I'm sure I'll be fine soon.'

She and Maureen had struck up a friendship in the time she had been there. Maureen was now doing the food shopping in town for her. Charity was afraid to venture there in case one of her Gypsy friends spotted her. It wouldn't do for her to be dragged back to the camp. She doubted her cousin would still want to marry her even if she was. She would be disgraced now and it was unlikely any Gypsy man would want her. Even so, she had no regrets. She was living for the time when she could be with Luca again.

Maureen arrived almost an hour later. Charity had dressed the children by that time and now they were happily playing outside.

Maureen put the two baskets of groceries on the table and stared at her. 'Feeling all right, are you?' she asked, much as Eddie had earlier.

'I'm just feeling a bit off colour. A bit sick that's all,' Charity told her.

Maureen furrowed her brow. 'I see. Are you due to start a course?'

Charity thought about it for a moment and frowned. 'Actually, now you've mentioned it, I think I'm late,' she admitted.

'I see, and are they usually on time?'

'I'm usually as regular as clockwork,' she admitted. "But it's probably all the stress.' And she looked worried.

Maureen said nothing as she began to unpack the baskets. She hoped that Charity was right, for her sake.

‘I just heard in the shop that the circus should be here during the next week,’ she said.

Charity’s face lit up. Every hour would bring Luca closer to her now. She could hardly wait.

Chapter Eleven

As the circus pulled onto a field on the outskirts of Appleby, a cheer went up. The townsfolk looked forward to its visit every year. Luca and the circus folk were exhausted after the long journey, but there was no time to rest just yet. Their first priority would be getting the animals unloaded from the wagons and into suitable enclosures, and then they'd be erecting the big top. It would need to be ready for the first performance the following day.

The day passed in a blur for Luca. He wanted to seek out their Gypsy friends and see if Charity had managed to escape, but that would have to wait until much later. If she had he would have to look surprised when he heard about it. It wouldn't do if her family realised he already knew.

As he led the horses down a ramp from the wagon, Scarlet appeared. He sighed. At least he had had a break from her during the journey.

'Why don't you come and have dinner with us when you've settled the animals?' She batted her eyelashes at him.

‘Thanks, but I’ll be fine,’ he told her shortly.

A flash of annoyance crossed her pretty face. None of her womanly wiles seemed to be working on him.

‘But you must eat,’ she persisted. ‘And mother is cooking a rabbit stew. You like that.’

Luca sighed. ‘Very well, could you perhaps save some for me? But I don’t know what time we’ll be finished.’

Satisfied, she nodded before suggesting, ‘Could I help you?’

He shook his head. ‘I don’t think you’d be much good at erecting the big top, do you?’

‘Probably not.’ She giggled. ‘Just come to our trailer when you’re finished.’ And with that she floated away.

It was late evening before the work was finished. By bedtime all the fairground rides had been erected, the big top was standing proud against a starry sky and the coconut shy and the other stalls were ready to receive their first visitors. The animals had also been fed and bedded down.

Luca stretched wearily as he wiped sweat from his brow. It had been a long, hard day and he ached everywhere. He briefly thought of going straight to his own trailer to sleep, but he realised that if he did Scarlet would only come looking for him. Anyway,

Charity had told him that she would get word to him of where she was through Scarlet so he didn't want to risk upsetting her. So, with a sigh he headed to her parents' trailer. She was sitting on the steps with the stew pot keeping warm on a fire in front of it.

'There you are!' She jumped up, setting her bright skirt swirling about her slim legs. 'I was just about to come and find you.' She quickly ladled some curry into a dish and handed it to him with a spoon.

He could hear her parents and siblings in the trailer behind her but they didn't join them.

'Would you like some more?' she offered sweetly when he had finished.

'No thanks. I'm off to bed.' He handed the dish back and turned to leave. 'But thanks for the supper.'

She pouted. 'Couldn't you stay a while longer? My father has some ale in the barrel under the trailer. You must be thirsty after all your hard work.'

He shook his head and without another word strode away. Once back in his own trailer, he quickly undressed and fell into bed, but sleep eluded him, despite how tired he was. He longed to head for the Gypsy camp, but he would have to be patient.

Late the following evening, when the last of the fair visitors had left, Luca, his father and some of the circus men set off for the camp. The Gypsy men were sitting around the fire drinking ale. Jethro, Charity's father, instantly rose to clap Rory on the back when he saw him.

'Welcome, my friend, how are you?' His loud voice carried around the camp.

'I am well, Jethro, and yourself?'

Jethro sank back onto the grass with a shake of his head. 'We are very worried,' he admitted. 'Our daughter Charity has disappeared.'

Luca was glad of the darkness as it hid the colour that rose in his cheeks. So, she had done it. Charity had made her escape.

'What do you mean – she's disappeared?' Rory was horrified.

Jethro shrugged. 'Just that my friend. We all went to bed and when we woke the next morning she was gone.'

'But why would she do that? Have you tried to find her?'

'She left a note saying that she had formed an attachment with a young man not of our choosing so felt she must leave. I do not know why she would do such a thing,' Jethro told him. 'And yes, we have tried to find her but with no luck. Her mother is distraught. It is as if she has vanished into thin air. Her mother thinks it may be because I was about to announce her engagement to her cousin. She did not seem keen on him, but that is the way we do things – a girl will always marry a man of her parents' choosing. It is a great disgrace for a Gypsy girl to run away. I fear she might be with another young man. And if that's the case, when I find them, he will wish for death.'

Luca gulped. Jethro didn't sound like he was joking.

Rory began to pour some tankards of ale and passed them around. Very soon they were getting merry, but Luca needed to keep his wits about him. After all, it would be here that Charity would seek Scarlet out to tell him where she was and when she did he would have to move quickly to get away. He could hardly wait.

Chapter Twelve

The next few days were painful for Charity. Knowing that Luca was so close was a sweet torture. Even so, she knew that she must choose her moment to find Scarlet carefully. She was afraid of going into town. Even more afraid of venturing anywhere near the Gypsy camp for fear of being seen. And what excuse could she make to Mr Wells for sneaking out late at night?

The perfect opportunity presented itself when Maureen came to the farm one day. She told Charity that Eddie had asked if she would like to go with him and the children to the circus. He had kindly invited Charity too but she had declined as she couldn't be seen by any of the circus folk.

'It's been years since I went to one,' Maureen confided happily. 'In fact, I was only a little girl.'

Charity smiled at her. Maureen was such a lovely person.

'A night out will do you good.' Charity said. 'What were you thinking of wearing?'

Maureen looked bemused. 'Wearing? Why, what's wrong with what I have on?'

'Absolutely nothing if you're working,' Charity told her tactfully. 'But perhaps we could find you something a little more colourful for an evening out. And you could wear your hair loose too. I bet it's really pretty when it isn't tied back. Come on, let's go and look in Mary's trunk. Eddie did tell you to help yourself.'

Maureen self-consciously touched the unbecoming bun on the back of her head. She couldn't remember the last time she had worn her hair loose.

They sifted through the clothes in the trunk and eventually Charity lifted out a dress. 'Look at this. It would be perfect for a night out at the circus.' It was cream cotton sprigged with small blue forget-me-nots.

Maureen sighed. 'Oh, I remember Mary wearing that.' She looked sad.

'What actually happened to her?' Charity asked. She had never liked to ask Eddie.

'She died when having their last child and the baby passed away as well. It was a little boy.' Maureen shook her head as she remembered. 'The last thing she said to me was, "Look after them for me, Maureen." And I have tried to. But I can't do as much as I'd like with Mother being so ill. Still, he has you now.'

‘Yes, but I won’t be here forever. Sadly, neither will your mother,’ Charity answered. ‘But now try this on. We can soon alter it if we need to. We can wash and iron it and freshen it up as well.’

Maureen slipped out of her drab outfit and into the dress. Charity turned her to look in the cheval mirror.

‘Just look at yourself. You’re beautiful. And the dress fits as if it was made for you.’

Maureen blushed. She’d never considered herself to be beautiful. But she had to admit she did look very different in the dress.

‘Right, that’s you all sorted,’ Charity said happily. But then a wave of nausea made her clap her hand across her mouth.

As she made a run for the door, Maureen frowned. It was beginning to look horribly like her suspicions might be correct.

The following night there was great excitement in the farmhouse. Charity was getting the children ready to go to the circus, Eddie was upstairs getting changed and Maureen was due to arrive any minute.

After a while, Eddie came down in a clean shirt and trousers. His hair was still wet and seeing how happy the children were, he smiled.

‘You look very smart,’ Charity commented.

Seconds later, the back door opened and Maureen appeared. Eddie and Charity gaped at her. She looked so different she was almost unrecognisable. The dress seemed to emphasise the colour of her eyes and her fair hair was loosely curled about her shoulders, making her appear much younger.

'Why . . . you look grand,' Eddie told her shyly and she blushed.

'And so do you,' she answered as the children ran to cuddle her.

'Come along then, else you'll miss the beginning,' Charity told them.

Eddie smiled as he ushered the children towards the door and finally, Charity was alone. She had told Eddie that she was going to go for a long walk. But really she intended to head to the circus camp and wait for a moment when she could catch Scarlet alone. And then . . . Her heart beat faster. Once Scarlet had told Luca where she was, he would come to her and they could begin their life together.

She waited for half an hour before taking up her shawl and leaving the farmhouse. She remembered where the circus stayed each year and was sure she would have no trouble finding it. It was next to a large wooded area where she could hide until it got dark. All she would have to do was keep an eye out for Scarlet then.

By the time she came to the edge of the woodland the circus had begun. She could hear the crowd inside laughing at the antics of the clown. Her heart was racing as she peeped out from behind the shelter of a tree. She had chosen to wear the drab clothes she wore for cleaning. Her hair was pulled into the nape of her neck and tied with string. If anyone noticed her they would think she was one of the village girls. Eventually, the evening darkened as she kept a close eye out for Scarlet. She was hoping for a glimpse of Luca as well but there had been no sign of him. Finally, the circus came to an end. The crowd began to pour out of the big top and head for the fair.

And that was when she spotted her. Keeping to the shadows, she made her way towards her.

'Psst . . . Scarlet!'

Scarlet looked around. As she spotted Charity hurrying towards her, she frowned.

'Scarlet, you may have heard that I've run away?'

Scarlet nodded.

'Good, then I wondered if you would pass on a message to Luca so he can find me. We did tell you that we wanted to be together.'

She withdrew a piece of paper from her pocket and pressed it into Scarlet's hand. 'Will you give him this for me? It has the address of where I am on it.'

She noticed that Scarlet didn't look particularly happy to see her. In fact, she looked very ill at ease.

'Is everything all right?' Charity suddenly had a sinking feeling in the pit of her stomach. 'Is Luca well? Nothing has happened to him, has it?'

'No, and yes I will pass the letter on,' Scarlet said quietly as she slid the piece of paper into her pocket.

Charity went to hug her. They had always been friends, but for some reason Scarlet drew back.

'You'd best be going,' she advised uneasily, glancing around to make sure no one was watching them. 'Some of your people could be here tonight. It wouldn't do if you were to be seen.'

Charity nodded. She couldn't understand why Scarlet was being so cold towards her. 'Yes, you're right. Just tell Luca to come for me as soon as he can, please.'

Scarlet rushed away without another word as Charity turned to make her way back to the farm. She hadn't managed to see Luca, but still, once he had seen Scarlet he would know where she was. On this happier thought she hurried her steps.

Chapter Thirteen

Charity was in bed when the family arrived home that evening. She could hear their cheerful chatter downstairs. They had obviously enjoyed themselves and she was glad. It had been hard for the children since they had lost their mother.

The next morning, when Charity made her way downstairs, they were beaming at her as she entered the kitchen.

She smiled as she ushered them to the table for their breakfast. 'So, I take it you had a good evening.'

'Oh yes!' Simon's eyes lit up as he thought back to it. 'We saw all the animals in the circus. There were beautiful bears and dogs that danced. And there was a juggler and a lady who swung high up on a swing from the ceiling. And there were clowns and lots of other things too.' His words tripped over each other in his excitement to tell her all about it. 'Then when the circus was done Daddy and Maureen took us to the fair.' Little Tilly's head was nodding in agreement. 'We had a toffee apple and we went on some rides.'

'Oh yes, which ones did you go on?' Charity asked.

'First, we went on the swing boats. They went really high and Tilly was a bit frightened,' he told her with a grin. 'Then we went on this roundabout. It was all different coloured horses that went up and down. Tilly liked that one. We had a go on the coconut shy too. I didn't win one but Daddy did. He gave it to Maureen. And we saw a funny lady who had a beard and a man who only came up to the belt on Daddy's trousers.'

Charity smiled as she placed bowls of porridge in front of them. 'It sounds like it was a wonderful night.' It was lovely to see them both so happy.

Eddie entered the kitchen then and he too seemed in a good mood.

'I gather the evening went well?'

'It certainly did,' he agreed as he ruffled the children's hair. He had been out feeding the pigs. He hastily washed his hands at the sink and Charity served him his breakfast. They were getting into a routine now and she felt a little guilty. If everything went to plan, she might not be there for much longer unless Eddie could find work for Luca too. If he couldn't they would have to move on and she just hoped the family would cope well without her. But then the nausea she had been suffering returned.

With a hasty apology, she hurried out to the lavatory in the yard. This was occurring every morning now, and yet by lunchtime she usually felt fine again and she felt seriously concerned now..

When she had finished her chores that morning she took the children for a walk. They wandered down to the brook.

'Can we take our shoes off and have a paddle?' Simon asked and she nodded. Soon the children were happily splashing. She had grown very close to them in the few weeks she had been there. She knew that she would miss them when she left but it couldn't be helped. She wondered if Scarlet had delivered her note to Luca yet. Her heart raced at the thought of it. He could turn up at any time now, and as much as she knew she would miss the children, he couldn't come quickly enough.

The next morning, when Maureen appeared, she found Charity coming out of the lavatory.

'Have you been sick again?' she asked.

Charity nodded as she wiped her hand across the back of her mouth. 'Yes, it happens every morning now.'

'And has your course come yet?'

Charity shook her head.

'Then I think it's time we had a little chat. Come on, we'll go in and I'll make you a nice cup of tea.'

Once they were in the kitchen Maureen sat down opposite her. The children had gone out to play so it seemed a good time.

'Have you had any other symptoms apart from the nausea and the missed course?' Maureen asked.

Charity paused as she thought for a moment. 'Only that my breasts have felt a little tender.' She blushed as she told her.

'And I know this is personal but I have to ask. Have you and your young man ever laid together?'

Deeply embarrassed, Charity looked down at her hands folded in her lap. Lying with a man before marriage was the most shameful thing a Gypsy girl could do. So why, she wondered, did she not regret it? The night she had given herself to Luca had felt so right.

She nodded. 'Yes, just once.'

'That's all it takes,' Maureen said wisely. She had never had children herself, but she had seen many village women who had. 'And I think from what you've just told me you could be expecting a child.'

Charity's head snapped up, her eyes huge. 'Surely not. After just one time?'

Maureen nodded.

'So what am I to do?' Charity began to panic. 'What will Luca say when I tell him?'

'I'm sure that if he loves you, he'll be pleased,' Maureen comforted her. Charity had told her everything about him now and he sounded a decent man. 'Have you managed to get word to your friend?'

Charity sighed. 'Yes, while you were all at the circus I snuck out. She didn't seem very pleased to see me though. But she did promise to get my message to Luca. He should have it by now.'

'There you are then.' Maureen patted her hand. 'I've no doubt he'll be turning up any time now.'

Feeling slightly better, Charity looked towards the window. Of course, Maureen was right. He could even arrive that very day. The thought of seeing Luca made her heart beat faster.

The following week passed painfully slowly for Luca. Charity had promised him that as soon as the circus arrived in Appleby, she would seek out Scarlet. Every day he went to find Scarlet but she always said the same thing: 'I've heard nothing!'

Something told him that all was not well. He knew from Charity's father that she had run away, so where could she be and why had she not sent word?

Each night he lay awake worrying. He would have liked to start searching for her, but he knew that if he did it would arouse suspicion. And so, he waited and waited. The funny thing was that suddenly Scarlet was avoiding him too. It was a relief in one way. At least she wasn't behind him every time he turned around now. Perhaps she had finally got the message that he wasn't interested? Yet somehow that didn't quite ring true. Scarlet was spoilt and used to getting what she wanted, so why her sudden change of heart?

One night, as he lay alone thinking of Charity, the door to his trailer slid open. Scarlet was standing there and before he could say a word she came to sit beside him.

'What are you doing?' He leaned up on his elbow. 'Get out, Scarlet. You know you shouldn't be here.'

'Why not?' she purred.

To his horror he saw that she was sliding her blouse off her shoulders. With a muttered oath he leapt off the bed, wrapping the sheet around himself.

'Aren't you tempted to make me yours?' she asked suggestively.

'No, I am *not*,' he said. 'And if your father catches you here, he'll kill us both.'

'Not if I tell him you took advantage of me,' she said spitefully. 'He'd see that you marry me then. Whether you want to or not.'

He glared at her. 'When are you going to get it into your head that it's Charity I love?'

She bounced to her feet, her eyes flashing. 'And when are you going to get it into your head that she doesn't want you? She would have come to find you by now if she did, wouldn't she?'

Taking her arm Luca steered Scarlet towards the door. 'She'll come,' he told her as he showed her out. 'Now leave me alone.' And with that he slammed the door on her and her wounded pride.

Furious, Scarlet adjusted her clothes and strode away. But she wasn't finished yet. She'd make him sorry for the way he'd treated her if it was the last thing she did.

Chapter Fourteen

'I hear the horse fair will be over next week,' Maureen told Charity two weeks later. 'The Gypsies will be moving on then.'

Charity wasn't sorry to hear it. She was almost afraid to step out of the door for fear of bumping into one of them. 'And what about the circus?'

'I believe they'll be here for another two weeks.' Maureen smiled. 'Tilly and Simon want to go again. They so enjoyed it.' It had been clear to Charity since being there how much Maureen adored the children. She thought it might be because she had never had children of her own. The week before Maureen's mother had taken a turn for the worse. It looked unlikely that she was going to recover this time.

Now Maureen glanced at Charity. The poor girl had dark circles beneath her eyes and she knew she wasn't sleeping well. She wasn't eating much either.

'Look, why don't you wait until the Gypsies have gone and go down to the circus again?' she suggested.

'Perhaps your friend hasn't managed to pass your message on to your young man yet.'

'I would have thought she'd have had time to see him by now,' Charity said quietly, remembering how cold Scarlet had been towards her. 'But I think you're right. That might be the best thing to do.'

Word reached them that the Gypsies had moved on late the following week. That evening Charity waited until Eddie and the children were in bed and slipped away. It was dark but the darkness held no fear for her. She knew that it would be much later before the circus folk got to their beds. When she reached the wooded area, she could see the men closing down the fair stalls. There was no sign of Luca so she waited. She was rewarded some minutes later when Scarlet appeared. Quickly pulling her shawl about her face Charity hurried over to her.

'Scarlet.'

Once again, the girl looked surprised to see her. Charity took her arm and drew her into the shadows.

'Did you manage to give the letter to Luca?'

Scarlet looked uncomfortable.

'Yes, I did . . . but . . .' Scarlet lowered her head. 'Look, there's no easy way to say this so I may as well just come out with it. The thing is, everything has changed since you ran away.'

'What do you mean changed?'

Scarlet looked ashamed. 'It was after you left that Luca and I . . . Well, we realised that we have feelings for each other. I'm so sorry, Charity. We never meant it to happen. But you must see that we're a better match than you two could ever be. We are both circus folk. Had you two got together it would have caused terrible trouble.'

Shock coursed through Charity as her hand flew to her mouth. She felt as if all the air had been sucked out of her. It couldn't be true, could it? Luca loved her, she was carrying his baby. And yet one look at Scarlet's face told her that it must be.

'Luca and I are betrothed now,' Scarlet went on and Charity felt as if a dagger had been plunged into her heart. 'Our people helped us celebrate our betrothal. I couldn't bring myself to tell you the last time we met. As I said, I'm so sorry. We never meant to hurt you.'

Charity gathered what pride she had left and stood tall. 'It's all right,' she said. 'I hope you'll both be very happy.'

For the first time Scarlet felt a flicker of guilt. It was her now who caught Charity's arm as she turned to leave. 'What will you do? Will you go back to your people?'

Charity shook her head. 'No, that is out of the question. They would never accept me back. I have shamed them by refusing to marry the man of their choosing and running away to be with another. But don't worry, I shall be quite all right. Goodbye, Scarlet. I doubt we will see each other again.'

With her head held high, Charity walked away. It was only when she reached the shelter of the trees that she stopped, and, sinking down onto the grass, she began to cry.

Back at the circus Luca hurried over to Scarlet. 'Who was that girl I just saw you talking to?' he asked. 'She was wearing drab clothes and had a shawl drawn about her head.'

'Oh her. That was just a girl from the village asking what time the first performance is tomorrow.'

'I see.' He frowned. He had already asked her countless times if Charity had left a note for him with her but the answer was always the same.

And yet, there had been something about the girl that had seemed strangely familiar. With a shrug he moved away and Scarlet smiled triumphantly as she watched him go. Hopefully, that would be the last they would ever see of Charity.

Chapter Fifteen

Charity had no idea how long she sat there on the grass. Eventually, the hooting of an owl brought her thoughts back to where she was. She felt numb inside as she stumbled to her feet. She knew that she must have been there for a long time. Her skirts were wet with dew and the circus camp was silent. She set off back to the farm. On the way, she passed the river where the Gypsies had washed their horses. Just for a moment she had a desire to throw herself in. How nice it would be to feel the cold water carrying her away. It would close over her head and the pain she was feeling would be gone. But then she thought of the life growing inside her. Her hand dropped to tenderly stroke her stomach. She was carrying Luca's child. That was all she would ever have of him now. She forced herself to move on and when she reached the farm she crept across the yard. Everybody would be asleep and she didn't want to disturb them.

Once she got to her room she hastily undressed and pulled her nightgown over her head. She was still trying to accept the fact that two people she loved had betrayed her. She and Scarlet had been friends for many years, Luca had been her first love. What was going to happen to her now? What would Eddie say when he found out that she was going to have a child? He'd probably send her packing and then where would she go? All her hopes and dreams were in ashes. She finally fell into an uneasy sleep with tears on her cheeks.

Two days later, Maureen came to the farm. She instantly saw that something was wrong with Charity but she bided her time before she asked. Only when the children were outside did she turn to Charity.

'So did you go to the circus to find your friend?'

'Yes, I did.'

'And?'

'And she told me that everything has changed. Since I ran away, she and Luca have become a couple. He loves her now.'

Maureen looked shocked. 'Surely not. You seemed so sure of him.'

Charity nodded. 'I was, but it seems I meant nothing to him. And now I don't know what I'm going to do. When Eddie finds out about the baby, he'll probably ask me to leave.'

'Let me speak to him for you,' Maureen urged. 'I've known him for a long time and he has a kind heart.'

Charity nodded. At least if Maureen could get Eddie to agree to her staying, she and her child would have a roof over their heads.

Down at the circus Luca was becoming worried. They had been camped there for some weeks now. Charity had promised to get in touch as soon as she knew they had arrived and it wasn't like her to break her word. He was becoming seriously concerned that something had happened to her. He finished feeding the animals and went to look for Scarlet. He found her outside her trailer and drew her out of earshot of everyone.

'Scarlet, are you quite sure that you haven't seen Charity?'

'Actually . . . I have,' Scarlet told him. 'The woman in the drab clothes you saw me speaking to the other night was Charity.'

'So why did you lie to me?' He frowned at her and she lowered her eyes.

'I didn't want to hurt you.'

'Hurt me?' He looked even more confused. 'What do you mean?'

She licked her lips. 'The thing is she came to tell me that . . .' She glanced up at him. The colour had drained from his face. 'That she's met someone else.'

'No!' He shook his head. 'I don't believe it. We love each other. That's why she ran away – so that we can be together.'

'I know but she found herself a job on a farm. And she said . . . Well, she said that she very quickly developed feelings for the farmer. She realised then that she'd made a mistake with you. She said to tell you that she was sorry. She never meant to hurt you. I think that she was thinking of her future. He can offer her a ready-made home whereas if you two were together I suppose it would be hard. I'm afraid she isn't the girl you thought she was, Luca.'

'But I would have done anything for her,' he said brokenly.

Scarlet gently stroked his arm. 'I know this must come as a shock. And I'm sorry that I didn't tell you straightaway. But I'm still here. I'll always be here for you, Luca.'

He stared at her for a moment before turning and walking away, his shoulders slumped. The bright future he had dreamed of with the woman he loved was gone now. And he didn't know how he would bear it.

Maureen managed to get Eddie alone later that day. Charity was collecting eggs from the barn when he entered the kitchen.

'Ah, Eddie, I need to have a word,' she told him gently and he nodded.

'Of course. Is everything all right? Your mother isn't worse, is she?'

'Actually, she is. But it isn't that I need to speak to you about. Come and sit down.'

He pulled out a chair and joined her at the table where she was shelling peas.

'So, what is it?' he queried.

'It's about Charity actually.' She went on to tell him about Charity running away to wait for her young man to join her. 'The thing is though, she's just found out that he's switched his affection to her friend. He won't be joining her now.'

'That's very sad,' Eddie said as he scratched his head. 'What a rotter. And she couldn't have been a very good friend either.'

'No, and that isn't the worst of it. You see Charity is going to have a baby and is now afraid that you'll throw her out. She'd have nowhere to go.'

'Oh dear!' He sighed before saying, 'I admit I wasn't thinking of having another child about the place when I took her on. But she is a good little worker. The children like her too.' He thought for a moment and then an idea came to him. 'How about we do up the little cottage at the other side of the orchard and Charity and the baby could live there? It's been empty for a while. That way she could carry on working here with the child.'

'I think that's an excellent idea.' Maureen was thrilled that he had been so understanding. He was such a good man. 'Shall I ask Charity how she feels about it?'

He nodded as he rose to go back to work. 'By all means. But now I must get on.'

Maureen smiled as she watched him leave.

Chapter Sixteen

'You mean he'll allow me to stay here?' Charity could hardly believe it when Maureen relayed what Eddie had said. She felt as if a huge weight was being lifted from her shoulders.

'He certainly will. I can take you to see the cottage if you like?' Maureen offered.

Charity nodded eagerly. At least now she would have a home for herself and her child. They set off soon after with Tilly and Simon running beside them. After passing through the orchard, Charity saw the cottage in a little clearing. The garden was overgrown but the cottage itself looked sturdy enough.

'It'll probably be very dusty inside,' Maureen warned as she took the key from her apron pocket. They entered a large kitchen cum sitting room and Charity looked around. As Maureen had said, it was very dusty but she liked it immediately. A small parlour led off this room and a staircase led to two bedrooms upstairs.

'We could have this cleaned and ready to move into in no time,' Maureen said as they moved from room to room. 'And there's an outside toilet and a wood shed just out there. Everything you need.'

'It's lovely,' Charity agreed. 'And so kind of Eddie to do this for me.' And yet deep down she dreaded living in one place. She had enjoyed her time on the farm because of Eddie's kindness. She had made a good friend in Maureen and she had grown fond of the children, but she missed life on the road and sometimes felt like a caged bird. Until now it was all she had ever known and she had loved it. She had imagined she and Luca in their own trailer moving from place to place. But that would never happen now. She would grow old here in her drab clothes. There would be no more bathing in the river. There would be no more dancing around the campfires. No more whittling wood into clothes pegs to sell in the villages they passed through. But she would have Luca's child and that would have to be enough.

Over the next few days, Charity spent every spare minute she had preparing the cottage. She cleaned the windows until they gleamed and washed the curtains. She polished the furniture until she could see her face in it. The floors were swept and mopped and cobwebs were dusted away.

Maureen made the old brass bed up for her with fresh sheets and blankets and Eddie fetched an old crib down from the attic for the baby. At last, her new home was ready to move into.

On the same day Maureen informed her that the circus had left the town. And on that day Charity's heart broke afresh. She could picture Luca with Scarlet sitting beside him as they took to the road. She tried to push the images aside but it was easier said than done. Even so, she was grateful to Eddie for giving her a place to live. Things would have been so much worse if he had turned her out.

'I've no doubt a pretty girl like you will find another love once the baby's here,' Maureen tried to comfort her.

Charity smiled sadly. She knew that what she had felt for Luca was a once in a lifetime love. It would never come again. From now on she would give all her love to his child.

Chapter Seventeen

The circus had reached Nottingham. As Luca helped erect the big top his heart wasn't in it. He usually enjoyed his job but now he felt empty. He had been so sure that he and Charity had a life together to look forward to. The one time they had come together had been so special, and there had been no regrets on either side. He loved her so much. Even giving up the circus to be with her had seemed a small price to pay. Now, he was struggling to understand how her feelings could have changed so quickly. She had never seemed to be a material person and he couldn't imagine her being happy staying in one place. She had loved her life on the road as much as he had. She had even left her family to be with him. So what could have changed her mind so quickly? But Scarlet had been adamant. He had studiously avoided her since she had passed on Charity's message. Now, he wondered if she was being entirely truthful. She had made no secret of the fact that she wanted him. Could she have lied to get him for herself?

He paused in the act of hammering in a tent peg and looked around. Scarlet was outside her trailer. As she saw him looking towards her, she tossed her head and frowned. Since not getting what she wanted from him her infatuation had clearly turned to disdain. He didn't mind that. At least she wasn't following him about anymore. He had even seen her flirting with some of the other circus men. With a shake of his head, he tried to concentrate on what he was doing, but it wasn't easy.

It was the middle of the afternoon when he knew what he must do. Tonight, he would speak to his parents and be honest with them.

His chance came late that evening as the last of the fair-goers trickled away.

'Mother, I need a word.'

Kezia was just about to enter her trailer but she turned to smile at him. 'Of course, Luca. Come in. I am just making cocoa for me and your father.'

Soon they were sitting together and they were watching him expectantly.

'So, what is so important that you need to talk to us about it so late?' his mother said encouragingly.

Luca sighed. He knew that what he was about to say would break their hearts. All his life he had been training to become the circus master when his father retired. But that would never happen now. His need to find Charity was too great. And so, he began to tell them about his love for her.

'But you know that the Gypsies and the circus people marry their own kind.' His father looked shocked.

'And we have always wondered if you and Scarlet would wed,' his mother added.

Luca shook his head. 'I'm sorry. But love strikes where it will. We have no choice in it.'

His mother sighed. 'You do realise that by running away Charity has shamed her family? It is highly unlikely they will accept her back now. That is, if she wanted to return to them.'

'I know that.' Luca sighed. 'But I have to try. I need to know that what Scarlet told me was true. I hope you understand.'

His father began to get upset and angry. 'So you are going to go on a wild goose chase looking for a girl who has already spurned you? Is she worth risking what you have worked for all your life? In a few years' time you could be master of all this. And what will we tell everyone if you leave? We will be a laughing stock.'

'Does that mean you will not let me come back?' Luca asked quietly.

His father opened his mouth to answer but his mother butted in first.

'There will always be a place here for you, my son.'

'Not if he brings the Gypsy girl back with him.' His father glared at her. 'What would people say?'

'Times are changing,' she said hotly. 'And if the only way I can have my son here is with her . . .' She paused. 'Then so be it.' She turned to Luca again and touched his hand gently before saying, 'Go and do what you have to do, and with my blessing. And remember, your home is with us, wherever we are.'

Luca gave her a kiss on the cheek and left quietly. It was time to start packing up his trailer. There was no time like the present.

Chapter Eighteen

Late in July Maureen didn't appear for work at the farm one day. Charity was concerned. The week before Maureen had confided that her mother was now gravely ill. She mentioned it to Eddie when he came in for a cup of tea mid-morning. He had been up all night with a sick cow and looked tired.

'I hope she's all right.' He frowned. 'I wonder if I should pop into town and see her?'

'I could go,' Charity offered. She didn't mind going into town now that her people had moved on. 'I could take the children with me. I have some shopping I need to get anyway. We're almost out of flour.'

He nodded. 'Thank you. I should be here when the vet arrives. I think old Daisy might be on her last legs.' He sighed. Daisy was one of his best milkers. She had been at the farm for years and he was fond of her.

So, shortly after, Charity tidied the children and they set off for the town. The children always enjoyed going, especially if Charity treated them to a sugar mouse each from the sweet shop.

Thankfully, Charity's morning sickness had abated now, but she had noticed her waistline was thickening. She had spent the night before letting the waistbands on her skirts out, but they were still slightly tight. Soon she would treat herself to some material and make some loose dresses. She had settled well into the cottage. She enjoyed the solitude of living alone but she still missed Luca desperately. She would often stand in the window wondering where he was and what he was doing. And then she would picture him with Scarlet. He would be kissing her as he had once kissed Charity. Then the pain of betrayal would come back tenfold. She had calculated that the baby would come sometime in late January to early February. She felt nervous at the thought of the birth without her mother to help her, but Maureen had promised that she would be there for her. Eddie had also promised to organise the midwife from the village nearer to the time.

It was a beautiful day. The sun was riding high in a cloudless blue sky. As they approached the high street in the small town, the children became excited. They loved to peer into the shop windows. Charity quickly got the shopping they needed before taking them to the sweet shop. Simon chose a sugar mouse and Tilly opted for a liquorice twist. And then they headed for Maureen's house. It was a small terrace where the doors opened directly onto the street. Some little girls were rolling hoops along the cobbles or playing hopscotch. The boys were kicking about an inflated pig's bladder that served as a football.

When they came to Maureen's door Charity tapped on it. She didn't want to make too much noise in case her mother was asleep. Maureen opened it almost immediately. She looked tired and drawn but she smiled at the sight of them.

'Come on in.' She held the door wide. 'I was just about to make a cup of tea. And I bet you two wouldn't say no to a glass of lemonade.'

The children skipped out to look at the yard and Charity asked, 'How is she?'

Maureen sighed. 'The doctor came this morning.' She blinked back tears. 'He said her heart is failing now. It could happen anytime.'

'I'm so sorry.' Charity knew how much Maureen loved her mother.

'Death comes to all of us be we beggars or kings,' Maureen said quietly. 'But how are you? I'm sorry I couldn't leave her today.'

'Oh, don't worry about that, and I'm fine,' Charity assured her. 'The morning sickness has all but stopped now.'

They stayed for another ten minutes. The children were becoming restless by that time so they set off for the farm again. 'How is she?' Eddie asked when they were home and he came in for his lunch.

'She looks tired and her mother is failing.'

He shook his head. 'Maureen has devoted her life to caring for her mother and her family since her father died. And she's been wonderful to me since I lost Mary. She's a good woman.'

Charity nodded in agreement.

Maureen sent word three days later that her mother had passed away peacefully in her sleep.

Eddie immediately stopped what he had been doing to go to her. When he came back, he told Charity. 'I have asked Maureen to move in here to be with us.'

'Oh, I see.' Charity had been hoping he would say that. But it did make her wonder where that would leave her.

He instantly put her mind at rest when he said next, 'I think there's more than enough work here to keep you both busy.'

Charity stifled a sigh of relief. She just hoped that one day Maureen and Eddie would realise they had feelings for each other. They were both good people and deserved a happily ever after.

Chapter Nineteen

'We're going to be busy,' Eddie said over breakfast one day in early September when the harvest was about to begin. Farmers from nearby farms would be arriving to help. They also employed people who were seeking casual work. 'If you two could organise sandwiches and bottles of tea it would be grand,' he said to Charity and Maureen.

'We'll bring them up to the top field for you at lunchtime.' Maureen had settled in as if she had always been there. The children adored her, and she and Eddie were growing closer by the day.

The only thing Charity was concerned about was the Gypsies. What if her own family came. She didn't know how she would face them. Especially when they realised she was going to have a child. But as Maureen pointed out, there was no point in worrying about something that hadn't happened yet.

Mid-morning they began to make a pile of sandwiches and load them into baskets. Other baskets were filled with bottles of cold tea. Then they all set off for the top field. The workers were ready for a break. It was a hot day and they were all hungry and thirsty. Many of them were bare-chested and sweating, their scythes flashing in the sunlight. There were some Gypsies there but none that Charity recognised. Relieved, she deposited the baskets and hurried back to the farmhouse. But unknown to her one pair of eyes followed her closely.

Luca had arrived there the night before. He had been searching for Charity ever since he had left the circus, but with no luck so far. He was right at the top end of the field, but there was something about the back of the girl he had just seen that looked wonderfully familiar. He couldn't see her face but her long black hair was identical to Charity's. She also had Charity's way of walking. He kept her fixed in his sight until she disappeared into the farmyard. His heart was thumping. Could this be the farm and the farmer she had left him for? Luca had met Eddie the night before and liked him. He had agreed Luca could park his horse and trailer at the edge of the bottom field. Now, Luca quickly made his way to the refreshments where

Maureen was handing out sandwiches. He smiled as he took one from her and accepted a bottle of cold tea.

'The girl that was here a few minutes ago,' he said casually. 'I think I recognised her from somewhere.'

'Who, Charity?' Maureen shook her head. 'I doubt it, she's not from around these parts. I've sent her in out of the sun. She's having a baby so we don't want her getting ill.'

Luca felt the colour drain from his face. Having a baby? He rushed off to find shelter in the hedgerow. There he sat feeling as if his heart was breaking. She had certainly wasted no time in forgetting him. He had thought that she would be the mother of his children, that they would grow old together. Now here she was wed to another and carrying his child. He supposed he couldn't blame her. It was a grand farm and Eddie was decent from what he'd seen of him. Somewhat older than Charity, admittedly, but he didn't suppose that mattered. She would be set for life now. Eddie had been able to offer her so much more than he could. There didn't even seem any point in speaking to her now. He considered downing tools and setting off to find the circus, but common sense told him that would be foolish. If he finished the job, he would earn enough to keep himself on the journey back.

He pushed the sandwich into the hedgerow – he wasn't hungry anymore – and went back to work.

Maureen watched him go with a frown on her face. He had seemed upset when she told him about Charity's baby. Why would that be? she wondered. With a shrug, she lifted the empty basket and went back to the farm.

'I just spoke to a young man who thought he might know you.' Maureen glanced at Charity out of the corner of her eye.

Charity was washing the dirty pots up at the sink. 'Oh yes. Who was he then?' she asked, panic creeping in that she'd been recognised.

'He didn't say his name but he was a handsome young chap.'

As a thought occurred to Charity her heart began to thud. 'What did he look like?'

Maureen paused to remember. 'He was tall, dark haired. Quite muscly.'

'He's probably mistaken me for someone else,' Charity said quietly as she stared from the kitchen window.

The man fitted Luca's description, but why would he be here now? He had chosen Scarlet and they would surely be travelling with the circus? She got on with what she was doing and tried not to think about it.

That was easier said than done, though. That night she found it hard to sleep and tossed and turned. Then she made her decision. She would take the sandwiches to the top field again the next day. Maureen could point the young man out to her then. It probably wouldn't be Luca but she had to know.

Chapter Twenty

It was another beautiful day, perfect for harvesting. Maureen and Charity prepared the sandwiches and tea and set off to take them to the workers.

'If you see the young man that thinks he knows me, could you point him out?' Charity said it casually but her heart was pounding.

Maureen glanced at her and nodded. Charity had been very quiet all morning.

As they approached the field, the men downed their tools and approached them. It was hard working in the hot sun and they were all ready for a break.

Luca saw Charity almost at once and hung back. But at the same instant Charity spotted him and a lump rose to her throat. They stared at each other for a moment before Luca moved forward.

'Hello, Charity . . . You're looking well.'

She nodded. 'So are you.'

'I hear you're going to be a mother,' he said next, and she nodded again. He looked so handsome she could hardly bear to look at him.

'Then I hope all goes well for you. The farmer is a good man.'

She could hardly believe what she was hearing. She was carrying his child and yet he seemed not to care. But then why would he? He had made his choice. Scarlet was probably waiting in their trailer for him even as he spoke. But why was he here and not travelling with the circus? It was all very strange.

'Thanks, yes, he is. And how is Scarlet?'

He looked surprised. 'She was fine the last I saw of her.'

'Good. Well, I must get on.' She turned to hurry away, unable to look at him for a moment longer. She knew if she did, she would break down and make a fool of herself.

Maureen was watching them curiously and as Charity passed her, she saw that she was upset. She frowned. There was something strange going on here and she intended to get to the bottom of it. She waited until Luca approached her for his sandwiches before asking, 'You do know Charity then?'

He nodded but she saw that he looked troubled. 'Yes, I do.' And without another word he went to sit in the shade of the hedgerow.

When Maureen got back to the kitchen, she saw instantly that Charity had been crying. She didn't immediately comment but instead filled the kettle to make a cup of tea.

'Is everything all right?' she asked after a time.

'Yes, fine.' Without another word, Charity lifted an empty basket and went to gather the eggs in.

Late that evening, when Eddie and the children had retired to bed, Maureen glanced at Charity. They were enjoying a last hot drink before retiring themselves. 'Is that young man, the one you spoke to today, the baby's father?' she asked bluntly.

Charity almost choked on her cocoa. For a moment Maureen thought she wasn't going to answer her.

But then Charity nodded miserably. 'Yes, he is.'

'I thought as much. And from the way he looked at you he still loves you.'

'So why is he with Scarlet and not me then?' A hint of angry colour had crept into Charity's cheeks. It always did when she thought of Luca's betrayal.

Seeing that she had upset her, Maureen said no more.

The next morning, before the family and Charity were up, Maureen walked to the bottom field. She stared at Luca's trailer. His old horse was cropping the grass outside and all was quiet. She waited patiently and soon after he appeared, knuckling the sleep from his eyes. As he spotted her, he looked mildly surprised.

'Good morning,' she greeted him. 'I thought I'd come out a little early and gather some mushrooms for breakfast. I don't suppose you'd care to join us?'

He shook his head. 'Thank you, but I don't think Charity and her husband would be too keen on seeing me there.'

Maureen feigned innocent surprise. 'Charity's husband? But she doesn't have one.'

He looked confused. 'But I thought she was married to Eddie, the farmer.'

Maureen shook her head. 'Oh no, Charity just works for him.'

Luca scratched his head. 'But the baby?'

'Oh, her young man let her down apparently.'

Hardly able to believe what he was hearing, Luca stared at Maureen incredulously.

Her words had the desired effect. Before she could say another word, he began to stride towards the farmhouse. She smiled. She could do no more.

When Luca arrived at the door of the farmhouse he tapped on it and strode in, and there was Charity washing pots at the sink.

'Luca!' She looked shocked. 'What are you doing here?'

'I could ask you the same. Scarlet told me that you had married a farmer and that you didn't want me any more!'

'But she told me that you and she had got together and . . .'

They stared at each other in shock as they realised what Scarlet had done to them. And then suddenly he was across the room and she was in his arms. Everything was right with the world again.

'As if I could ever love *anyone* but you,' he breathed as he rained kisses on her face, and she snuggled into him. 'And to find out that I'm going to be a father, it's wonderful!'

His lips came down on hers then and there was no more talk for some time.

It was almost an hour later when Maureen returned to find the young couple beaming.

'I'm afraid Scarlet lied to both of us,' Charity told her.

'Yes, she did. And when she found I still wasn't interested in her she transferred her feelings towards another of the circus chaps.'

Luca looked adoringly at Charity. 'Had it not been for you we might never have realised what she'd done.' He gave Maureen a grateful smile. 'So, you must be the first to know. I have asked Charity to be my wife and she has agreed.'

Maureen clapped her hands with delight. 'Why that's wonderful. When is the big day to be?'

'Just as soon as I can get the local vicar to marry us.'

'I'm so pleased for you. But I'd ask you both just one thing. Once you are married, please visit your folks. It might just be that they'll want to be part of their grandchild's life. If they don't you can always come back here and live in the cottage. I'm sure Eddie would be glad of another pair of hands to help about the place.'

Charity and Luca were married four weeks later in the tiny village church in Orton. Eddie and Maureen were their witnesses and the happy couple looked ecstatic.

Maureen had laid on a small tea party back at the farm for them once the service was over and it was there that Eddie made an announcement.

'First of all, I'd like to drink a toast to the happy couple.' He raised his glass of home-made wine and they all sipped. 'And secondly, Maureen and I would like to share a little news of our own.' He smiled at

Maureen fondly and she blushed prettily. 'I have asked Maureen to be my wife and I'm delighted to say she has agreed. Love must be in the air!'

Charity and Luca were thrilled for them. One way and another it had been a very happy day.

Chapter Twenty-One

'Come on, my love. Just one more good push and this baby should be here!' Charity's mother encouraged. It was a bitterly cold day in late January.

Thankfully, because they were such good friends, the two sets of parents had held a meeting when they discovered that the young couple were now married, after each receiving letters from Luca. And although it went against tradition, each set had agreed that they should be given a second chance and be accepted back into the fold. As Luca would be running the circus one day it made sense for them to return there where they now had their own trailer.

Outside, Charity's father and Luca's parents were pacing the ground outside the couple's home. They were anxiously waiting for the arrival of their first grandchild.

Charity's Gypsy family was parked in the next field to the circus in Nuneaton.

Luca felt as if the baby was never going to come and couldn't keep still. 'Surely it should be here by now,' he said to his father.

'Babies have a habit of coming when they're good and ready. But it shouldn't be much longer now,' his father soothed him.

Then suddenly the sound of a new-born baby's cry rent the air and Luca stopped in his tracks.

Seconds later the trailer door burst open and Charity's mother told him, 'You have a fine healthy son, Luca. And he looks just like you. Would you like to come in and see him?'

As Luca moved towards the steps, Charity's father sprinted away to tell the rest of the Gypsies the good news.

Back at the trailer, Luca approached the bed and gazed down at his wife and son in awe.

Charity looked worn out but she was glowing with happiness as the new father took the baby in his arms.

'I thought we might call him Noah,' she suggested.

'Noah?' He thought about it for a moment before nodding in agreement. 'Yes, it's a good name and it suits him. How are you, my love?'

'I'm tired but I've never been so happy.'

The door burst open and both sets of parents pushed in, keen to glimpse their new grandson.

Once, Luca and Charity had feared they could never be together, but love is a funny thing and had overcome all the obstacles. The union of the young couple from two different ways of life had brought about the blessing of a beautiful baby boy. And now they all had the rest of their lives to look forward to.

THE READING AGENCY | Quick Reads

About Quick Reads

"Reading is such an important building block for success"

– Jojo Moyes

Quick Reads are short books written by bestselling authors.

Did you enjoy this Quick Read?

Tell us what you thought by filling in our short survey. Scan the QR code to go directly to the survey or visit: **bit.ly/QuickReads2026**

Thank you to Penguin Random House, Hachette and all our publishing partners for their ongoing support.

A big thank you to Curtis Brown for supporting the 20th anniversary of Quick Reads.

A special thank you to Jojo Moyes for her generous donation in 2020–2022 which helped to build the future of Quick Reads.

Quick Reads is delivered by The Reading Agency, a UK charity that inspires social and personal change through the proven power of reading.

readingagency.org.uk **@readingagency** **#QuickReads**

The Reading Agency, Registered number: 3904882 (England & Wales)
Registered charity number: 1085443 (England & Wales)
Registered Office: 24 Bedford Row, London, WC1R 4EH
The Reading Agency is supported using public funding by Arts Council England.

Supported using public funding by ARTS COUNCIL ENGLAND

THE READING AGENCY **Quick Reads**

Find your next Quick Read

For 2026 we have 6 Quick Reads for you to enjoy:

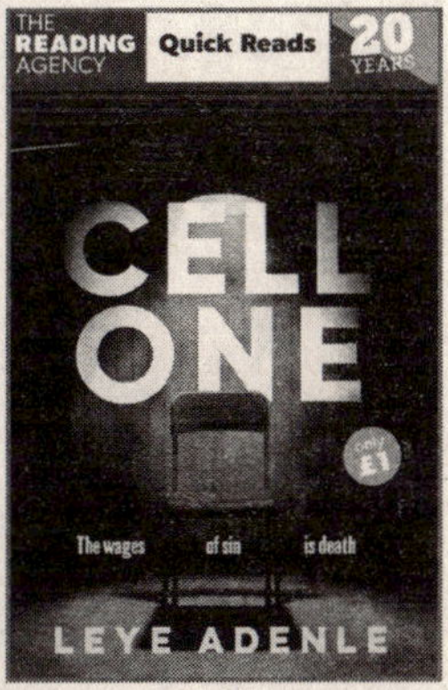

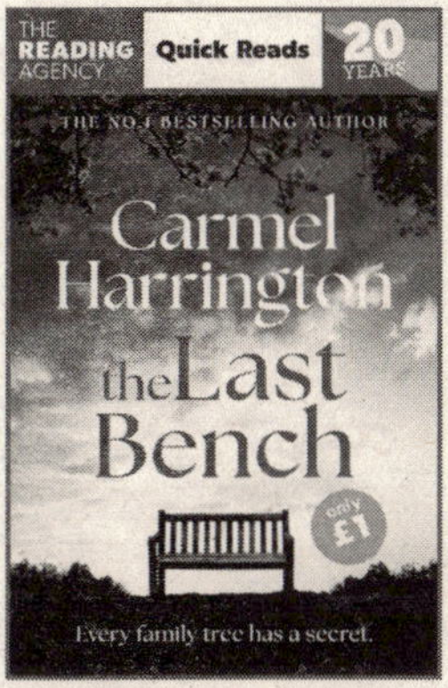

Quick Reads are available to buy in paperback or ebook and to borrow from your local library. For a complete list of titles and more information on the authors and their books visit: **readingagency.org.uk/quickreads**

Continue your reading journey with The Reading Agency:

Reading Ahead

Challenge yourself to complete six reads by taking part in **Reading Ahead** at your local library, college or workplace: **readingahead.org.uk**

Book Club Hub

Join the **Book Club Hub** to find a book club and discover new recommendations: **bookclubhub.co.uk**

World Book Night

Celebrate reading on **World Book Night,** every year on 23 April: **worldbooknight.org.uk**

Summer Reading Challenge

Read with your family as part of the **Summer Reading Challenge**: **summerreadingchallenge.org.uk**

For more information on our work and the power of reading visit: **readingagency.org.uk**

More from Quick Reads

If you enjoyed the 2026 Quick Reads, please explore our 6 titles from 2025:

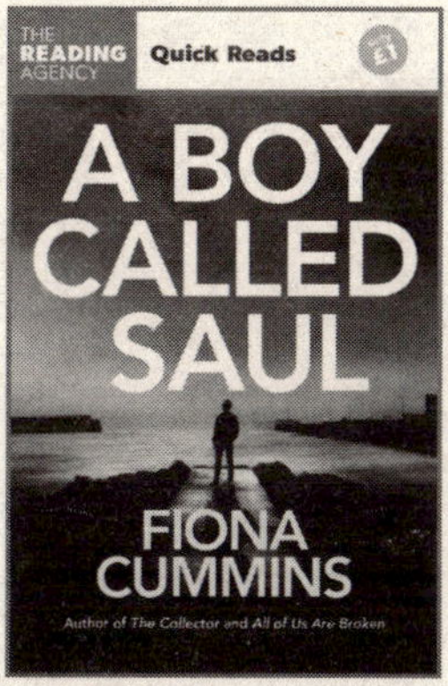

For a complete list of titles and more information on the authors and their books visit: **readingagency.org.uk/quickreads**

THE READING AGENCY

Also by Rosie Goodwin

The Bad Apple
No One's Girl
Dancing Till Midnight
Tilly Trotter's Legacy
Moonlight and Ashes
The Mallen Secret
Forsaken
The Sand Dancer
Yesterday's Shadows
The Boy from Nowhere
A Rose Among Thorns
The Lost Soul
The Ribbon Weaver
A Band of Steel
Whispers
The Misfit
The Empty Cradle
Home Front Girls
A Mother's Shame
The Soldier's Daughter
The Mill Girl
The Maid's Courage
The Lost Girl

The Claire McMullen Series
Our Little Secret
Crying Shame

Dilly's Story Series
Dilly's Sacrifice
Dilly's Lass
Dilly's Hope

The Days of the Week Collection
Mothering Sunday
The Little Angel
A Mother's Grace
The Blessed Child
A Maiden's Voyage
A Precious Gift
Time to Say Goodbye

The Precious Stones Series
The Winter Promise
An Orphan's Journey
A Simple Wish
A Daughter's Destiny
A Season for Hope
A Lesson Learned

The Flower Girls Collection
Our Fair Lily
Our Dear Daisy
Our Sweet Violet

The Rags to Riches Trilogy
The Rag Princess
One Woman's War

The Rags to Riches trilogy

Get to know Annie over the course of three books in a brand-new series from Rosie Goodwin

This Quick Reads Edition first published in the UK in 2026 by
ZAFFRE
An imprint of Bonnier Books UK
5th Floor, HYLO, 105 Bunhill Row,
London, EC1Y 8LZ

A CIP catalogue record for this book is available from the British Library.

ISBN: 978-1-80617-055-5

Also available as an ebook and an audiobook

1 3 5 7 9 10 8 6 4 2

Design and Typeset by IDSUK (Data Connection) Ltd
Printed and bound in Great Britain by CPI (UK) Ltd, Croydon CR0 4YY

MIX
Paper | Supporting responsible forestry
FSC® C013604
FSC www.fsc.org

The authorised representative in the EEA is
Bonnier Books UK (Ireland) Limited.
Registered office address:
Block B, The Crescent Building
Northwood, Santry
Dublin 9, D09 C6X8 Ireland
compliance@bonnierbooks.ie
www.bonnierbooks.co.uk